Horrible Harry and the Holidaze

Suzy Kline
AR B.L.: 3.5
Points: 1.0   LG

Something strange is going on . . . .

At the end of that day, Miss Mackle called Harry up to her desk. Although I couldn't hear what they were saying, I noticed Harry's eyebrows. They kept sinking lower and lower as he was talking to the teacher. It made him look mad, then sad. When it was Miss Mackle's turn to talk, Harry listened. Slowly he lifted his eyebrows higher and higher. None of us found out until later what it was all about.

BOOKS ABOUT
HORRIBLE HARRY AND SONG LEE

Horrible Harry
and the Holidaze

BY SUZY KLINE

Pictures by Frank Remkiewicz

PUFFIN BOOKS

PUFFIN BOOKS
Published by Penguin Group
Penguin Young Readers Group,
345 Hudson Street, New York, New York 10014, U.S.A.
Penguin Books Ltd, 80 Strand, London WC2R ORL, England
Penguin Books Australia Ltd, 250 Camberwell Road,
Camberwell, Victoria 3124, Australia
Penguin Books Canada Ltd, 10 Alcorn Avenue,
Toronto, Ontario, Canada M4V 3B2
Penguin Books (N.Z.) Ltd, 182-190 Wairau Road, Auckland 10, New Zealand

First published in the United States of America by Viking,
a division of Penguin Young Readers Group, 2003
Published by Puffin Books, a division of Penguin Young Readers Group, 2004

3   5   7   9   10   8   6   4

THE LIBRARY OF CONGRESS HAS CATALOGED THE VIKING EDITION AS FOLLOWS:
Kline, Suzy.
Horrible Harry's holidaze/ by Suzy Kline ; illustrated by Frank Remkiewicz.
p.   cm.
Summary: Miss Mackle's third graders share December holiday
traditions—Christmas, Hanukkah, Kwanzaa, Three Kings Day, and
Korean New Year—with each other and with Harry's great
grandfather, who has just moved into a nursing home.
ISBN: 0-670-03642-0 (hc)
[1.Holidays—Fiction. 2. Schools—Fiction. 3. Nursing homes—Fiction.
4.Grandfathers—Fiction.] I. Remkiewicz, Frank, ill. II. Title.
PZ7.K6797 Hq 2003
[Fic]—dc21   2003000946

Puffin Books ISBN 0-14-240205-2

Printed in the United States of America

Here Comes Santa Claus
Words and Music by Gene Autry and Oakley Haldeman
© 1947 (renewed 1975) WESTERN MUSIC PUBLISHING CO.
All Rights Reserved. Used by Permission.

Special appreciation to my new editor, Catherine Frank, for her help with this story; to Mom who lovingly shares so many of the activities she does at Mansfield Center for Nursing; to my husband, Rufus, for his valuable insight; to my precious daughter Jennifer, for her enthusiasm and interest; to Jinhi Park Sohn, for her help with the Korean New Year; to my dear friend, Cindy Gelzinis and her class at Southwest School in Torrington, Connecticut, for doing research on head measurements; and to Regina Hayes for creating the title.

Other Books by Suzy Kline

Dedicated to my loving daughter Emily, who keeps the holiday spirit alive every day.

Contents

The "D" Word

My name is Doug and I'm in third grade. I write about what happens in Room 3B, but this holiday story was the hardest one to write. Something was the matter with my best friend Harry. I can only come up with one way to describe him that month. Harry was *in a daze*.

He didn't flash his white teeth. He didn't call Sid a squid. He wasn't interested in things that were slimy, hairy, or creepy. And he didn't seem to be in love with Song Lee anymore. Harry just wasn't his horrible self.

It all started one morning in early December. "Boys and girls," Miss Mackle said. "Today is an exciting day! We have a new student in our room, *and* a new class pet!"

Everyone looked at the new boy, then at the large pet cage. A white towel was draped over it.

"This is Yousef Hadad. Tell us about yourself, Yousef!" the teacher said.

Yousef wasn't shy. He spoke right up. "Call me ZuZu. That's a nickname for Joseph in Lebanese. Lebanon is a country on the Mediterranean Sea."

Miss Mackle pulled down the wall map and pointed to his homeland.

ZuZu smiled as he took the white

towel off the cage. "And this is JouJou. He's a tortoiseshell guinea pig."

Everyone oohed and ahhed. Song Lee clapped her hands. JouJou looked like one giant auburn, black, and white hairball.

"What does JouJou mean in Lebanese?" Miss Mackle asked.

"George," ZuZu answered. "I'm sure

glad you said I could keep him in class, Miss Mackle, I love animals. I know how to take good care of them."

"Well, we're happy to have JouJou in Room 3B. He's a holiday gift to all of us!"

I immediately looked over at Harry and put two thumbs up. But Harry wasn't even looking at JouJou! He was scribbling a bunch of empty circles! What was going on, I thought. Harry *loves* hairy things.

"Who would like to help ZuZu look after JouJou this week?" the teacher asked.

Song Lee raised her hand first. Although she's shy, she loves animals. Last year she brought three to our class: Chungju, a salamander; Bong, a water frog; and Yi, a hamster.

The rest of us waved our hands madly in the air, too. Except for Harry. He just looked mad.

For a while, I was the only person who noticed Harry was in a daze. Song Lee was too busy helping ZuZu.

"I can fill the water bottle," she said.

"I can get the wet and dry food out," ZuZu replied. "I brought carrots and potato peelings in baggies, but I keep the cereal in this can. It has a nice tight lid."

When I stopped by Harry's desk, he was still doodling. His scribbled circles looked like the Grand Canyon. "What's the matter with you?" I asked. "You look like a scowling statue."

Harry didn't answer, but he did move. He shrugged his shoulders once.

After lunch things got even busier. Miss Mackle wrote the word *holidays* on the blackboard and underlined the "s" ending. "We are so lucky this year!" she exclaimed. "Remember when I sent a letter to your parents asking about the winter holidays you celebrate at home? Well, I found out that Room 3B families celebrate five!"

"Five?" Sidney gasped. "I thought

there was just one holiday. Christmas."

Mary blew her bangs up in the air. She does that when she gets angry. "Haven't you ever heard of Hanukkah, Sid?"

"Or Kwanzaa?" Ida added.

"Or Three Kings' Day?" Dexter replied.

"Mother is going to help me share our Korean New Year's," Song Lee said softly.

Miss Mackle beamed. "Thanks to our parent volunteers *everyone* in our class will get to know five winter holidays this year!"

"My dad's coming this afternoon," Dexter blurted out. "Any minute now!"

Everyone cheered as Miss Mackle pushed a long table in front of the room. Then we waited politely.

As soon as we heard footsteps coming down the hall, we all looked over at the doorway. Even Harry. I was hopeful he might snap out of his daze.

Two Surprises for Three Kings' Day

The tall man who entered our room was carrying a huge cake and had a bag over his shoulders. I noticed he was wearing a T-shirt that had a guitar on it. Now I know why Dexter is such an Elvis fan.

"Boys and girls," the teacher said, "this is Mr. Sanchez, Dexter's father. He's going to tell us about a holiday his family celebrates."

"Three Kings' Day!" Dexter shouted out.

"That's right!" his father replied, setting his things down on the long table. "Three Kings' Day is celebrated all over Latin America, Spain, and other parts of Europe. Dex, why don't you tell the class about the things I brought."

We all watched Mr. Sanchez empty the contents of his bag: one shoe, six walnuts, a piece of coal, a bucket, and a framed picture.

Dexter picked up the framed picture first. "Actually, my family celebrates both Christmas and Three Kings' Day. This is a picture of the three wise men who visited the stable when Jesus was born. On January sixth, the twelfth day after Christmas, we believe they visit our house and bring gifts like

Santa Claus does. Only they don't leave them in Christmas stockings by the fireplace. They leave them in shoes. Some people leave their shoes by their bed. We leave them by the door."

"Man," Sidney said. "You get presents *twice*?"

Dexter beamed. "Yeah!"

"What if the present is Tinker Toys?" Sid asked. "How would it fit in a shoe?"

"It happens a lot," Dexter answered. "Last year the wise men left me an Elvis video, *Fun in Acapulco*, by the door. It was too big for my shoe."

"What about the walnuts?" Sid asked.

"Oh, we leave nuts and a bucket of water for the wise men's camels," Dexter explained.

"Do you leave them coal, too?" Mary asked.

"No," Dexter groaned. "That's what you get in your shoe if you've been bad all year."

Mary laughed. "That's like Christmas. I bet Harry finds coal in his stocking!"

When Harry didn't raise his fist or say anything, ZuZu did. "Mary, that's a mean thing to say."

"Yeah," Sid said with a big grin. He liked it when Mary got zapped. It didn't happen very often. Slowly she sank down in her seat. Room 3B had a new judge. ZuZu.

Miss Mackle's next announcement made things fun again. "Please take off one of your shoes and put it next to the doorway."

"Neat-o," Sid said. "We get to go barefoot."

"Not barefoot," the teacher objected. "Leave your socks on."

As soon as all the shoes were near the door, Mary held her nose. "It smells in here."

It didn't bother Song Lee. She giggled. She doesn't mind slimy or smelly things. That's one reason why Harry likes her.

"Close your eyes," the teacher said. "The Three Wise Men are coming!"

"But Miss Mackle, it's not January sixth," ZuZu objected.

"Good listening," the teacher replied. "I mean let's *pretend* that it's January sixth."

Everyone put their heads down on

their desk and closed their eyes except me. I wanted to see if Harry was peeking. He wasn't. Harry wasn't being horrible at all.

A few minutes later, Miss Mackle called, "Come and see the surprise in your shoe."

Sidney made a beeline for his sneaker. Mary was behind him holding her nose with two fingers. *Crayons!* she exclaimed in a nasal voice.

"These are flashy ones," I said.

Harry was the last one to walk over and empty his shoe.

"Did you see what kind they are, Harry?" Miss Mackle asked. "They're fluorescent."

"Yeah," Harry replied. "But I like my old crayon stubs better."

Miss Mackle lowered her voice. "Are you okay, Harry?" she asked. "You seem a little out of sorts."

Before Harry could answer, Sidney blurted out, "Hey, can we leave our shoes off all day?"

"No," the teacher replied firmly.

Sid made a face as he slipped on his

shoe. He didn't bother tying the long shoelaces.

"Thank goodness!" Mary gasped, unplugging her nose. "I can breathe again."

"Thank you for my crayons," Song Lee said softly.

"Thank you, Wise Men," ZuZu pretended.

"*Thank you!*" we all chimed in.

"Okay, boys and girls," Mr. Sanchez said. "Now it's time for the second surprise, the crown cake!"

Everyone watched Dexter's father lift the lid off the cake carrier.

"Look what's on top of the snowy icing!" Mary said. "Cherries and pineapples! They look like shimmering jewels."

"Look at the hole in the middle of

the cake," I said. "It looks like a crown."

"I bet it would fit my head perfectly." Sid chuckled. "I think I'll try it on."

"Sidney, you don't wear cake," ZuZu corrected. "You eat it."

"Lighten up, Zu. I was just kidding," Sid replied.

Dexter tapped his dad on the shoulder. "Can I tell them now? Can I?"

"Yes!" Mr. Sanchez said.

"There is something really special about the crown cake we eat on Three Kings' Day. It has one *surprise* baked inside. Whoever finds it will have a lucky year."

Many of us crossed our fingers.

But Harry? I couldn't believe it. He made prayer hands. He *really* wanted that surprise.

After everyone took a bite of the delicious creamy cake, we looked around to see who had it.

"I got it! I got it!" Sidney screamed as he jumped out of his seat, tripped on his long shoelace, and tumbled to the floor.

"Are you okay, Sid?" Miss Mackle asked.

"Of course I am," Sid replied as he stood tall holding the little surprise. "I'm gonna have a lucky year! I've got this!"

We all stared at the tiny clay doll. "You lucky dog!" Dexter cried out.

Harry made a fist, thumped it on his desk, and gritted his teeth. "If I had gotten that doll," he said, "it might have changed things."

Miss Mackle and Mr. Sanchez looked at Harry, then at each other. I wasn't the only one who wanted to know, *What was going on with Harry?*

Heads Up for Kwanzaa

At the end of that day, Miss Mackle called Harry up to her desk. Although I couldn't hear what they were saying, I noticed Harry's eyebrows. They kept sinking lower and lower as he was talking to the teacher. It made him look mad, then sad. When it was Miss Mackle's turn to talk, Harry listened. Slowly he lifted his eyebrows higher and higher. None of us found out until later what it was all about.

The next day, Ida was really excited because her mom was coming to school.

At one o'clock, Miss Mackle introduced her. "Boys and girls, welcome Mrs. Burrell!"

Everyone looked at Ida's mom. She was holding a large basket and wearing a turban, big gold earrings, and a long dress. "Hi, boys and girls," she said cheerfully.

Ida popped out of her seat and proudly stood next to her mom. "Kwanzaa is a celebration of our African American heritage and our future," Mrs. Burrell explained. "Dr. Maulana Karenga created Kwanzaa in 1966."

"This is going to be fun," Ida said. "Can I start now, Mom?"

"Yes," her mother answered.

Ida pulled a flag out of the basket. "This is our African American flag. The red band stands for our struggle for freedom. The black stands for the color of our people, and the green represents the land of Africa and our hope for the future."

Ida reached in the basket again. This time she pulled out a mat. "This is a *mkeka* (mm-KEH-kah). That's a Swahili word for a handwoven mat. It is an example of things we make by hand."

Mrs. Burrell nodded, then added, "It also shows that who we are and what we do are woven together."

When Ida pulled out a large candle-holder, her mother said, "Kwanzaa starts on December twenty-sixth and

lasts seven days, through January first. Each night we light a candle. This candleholder is called a *kinara*. It symbolizes our ancestors. See, it has seven candles in Kwanzaa colors: three red, three green, and one black one in the middle."

Mary raised her hand. "Kwanzaa must be like Hanukkah. We have a candleholder too. Only it's called a menorah and has two more candles. We light a new candle each night just like you do, but Hanukkah lasts eight days, not seven."

Miss Mackle clapped her hands. "I love it when you find connections between the different holidays!"

Ida clapped her hands, too, then continued. "Kwanzaa is like Christmas because we exchange presents on the seventh day. Our gifts are homemade or handed down from our families."

"However, unlike Christmas and Hanukkah," Mrs. Burrell explained, "Kwanzaa isn't a religious holiday. Each family celebrates Kwanzaa in its own way, but all families recognize the seven principles of Kwanzaa, called *Nguzo Saba*."

"Please say those words again," ZuZu asked.

Ida and her mother repeated them slowly so we could learn them. "En-GOO-zoh SAH-bah."

"En-GOO-zoh SAH-bah," we all chanted.

"Nguzo Saba." Ida unrolled a chart with the seven principles printed neatly on it:

Unity:
working together

Self-determination:
speaking for ourselves

Cooperative work:
solving our problems

Cooperative economics:
building our businesses

Purpose:
remembering traditions and values

Creativity:
improving our communities

Faith:
believing in our people, our parents, our
teachers, our struggle for equality

Next Ida took out two pies from the basket.

"On the sixth night of Kwanzaa, we have a big feast called *karamu* (kah-RAH-moo). Some of the things we eat are collard greens, catfish, black-eyed peas, corn, fruit, and sweet potato pie! We brought a sample for you!"

"Ooooh," we said, watching Mrs. Burrell serve the pie on paper plates.

"Mmm!" I said swallowing my first sweet bite. "This is goooooood."

"Can we have seconds?" Sid asked.

"I'm sorry, there isn't enough," Mrs. Burrell replied. "But we do have a special activity. Making *kufis*."

"What are *kufis*, Ida?" ZuZu asked.

"African hats," Ida answered. "First you have to measure the *circumference* of your head."

Ida's mother smiled at her when she said the "c" word correctly.

"We'll give everyone three strips of poster paper so you can make a skull cap hat," Ida said.

"Skull cap!" Sid repeated. "Neat-o!"

As soon as Ida gave everyone a tape measure from one of the plastic tubs in our math corner, we compared head sizes. Mary went first.

"Mine's twenty-one inches."

"Mine's fifty-eight inches!" Sid bragged. "I have the biggest head in the class."

ZuZu put down his tape. "Sidney, that couldn't be. Your head isn't five feet around."

"T-rex might have one that big, but not you," Harry piped in. That private talk with the teacher must have helped some. Not only was Harry making a hat, he was thinking about horrible things again, like dinosaurs.

"Look," Sid replied. "A brain the size of mine needs lots of room."

Miss Mackle smiled as she went over to Sid's desk. "I think you're using the metric side of your tape, Sidney. You're right though, your head does measure fifty-eight. Fifty-eight centimeters."

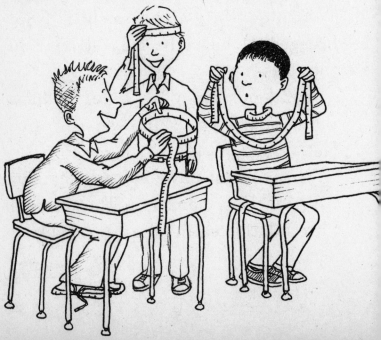

Sid flipped the tape over and remeasured. "Okay, it's twenty-three inches. Same thing. My head still is the biggest in the class."

Ida got us back on track. "Make your strips a little longer than your head size so the ends overlap when you staple them. One goes around your forehead. The other two crisscross on top and attach to it. You can draw shapes on the

strips with Magic Markers. After that, you can line the inside of your crown with any color of crepe paper you want."

"I'm using black," Mary said.

"I'm using red," Sid said.

"I'm using green," Song Lee said.

When we finished our *kufi* hats, we put them on and sat proudly together for a picture. I thought Mary's head looked bigger than Sidney's though. It probably was her pigtails.

Crash!

Wednesday Miss Mackle passed out permission slips that we had to take home and get signed by our parents.

"Yahoo! A field trip in December!" Dexter sang out. Then he drummed his fingers on a pretend guitar.

ZuZu read every word on the permission slip. "We're going to Shady Pines?" he asked. "Where is that?"

"Harry," Miss Mackle said. "Would

you like to explain the activity?"

"Sure," Harry said. "We're going to visit my great-grampa Sam Spooger. He—" Harry paused for a moment— "moved to Shady Pines. That's a nursing home four blocks from our school."

Miss Mackle walked over and put her hand on Harry's shoulder. "Harry and I thought a trip to Shady Pines

would be a great idea. We could visit the elderly people who live there and share some of our holiday activities."

So that's what put Harry in a daze! His great-grandfather wasn't living with him anymore. I knew he and Harry were buddies. He told him about Gremlins and World War II fighter planes. He was a hero during the war and saved lives. I knew he and Harry played poker a lot at home.

"We could share our favorite stories and poems. That's what we do at our house for Kwanzaa," Ida replied.

"I'll ask Mom if we can play the dreidel game," Mary suggested. "We always play that at Hanukkah."

"I could bring my Elvis 'Christmas Together' CD, and we could sing 'Here Comes Santa Claus,'" Dexter added.

"Wonderful!" Miss Mackle exclaimed. "So get your permission slip signed and bring it back this week. We're going Monday!"

The next morning we were all shivering in the playground waiting for the school bell to ring. It was sleeting again and really cold.

Suddenly a car skidded across the road, jumped over a curb, and crashed into the tall fir tree in front of Southeast School.

Bam!

Everyone screamed.

Seconds later, Mr. Cardini, the school principal, came running out of the building and ordered everyone inside. As we passed by the fence, we could see the old fir tree was slumped over.

I was really thankful the driver got

out of the car okay. He looked fine. His car didn't though. It had a smashed front fender. Mrs. Funderburke, the cafeteria lady, rushed outside. "I called nine-one-one," she yelled. "Come downstairs for coffee and cookies and get warm."

"I'm glad everyone's safe!" Miss Mackle said as we rushed into Room 3B.

"What a cool smash up!" Sid said. "Bam! Wham! Crash!"

"That's a terrible thing to say, Sidney," ZuZu snapped.

"It sure is!" Mary agreed. I had a feeling she and ZuZu were going to be great friends.

Harry was pressing his nose against the window. Since we were on the second floor, we could see every-

thing. Even the skid marks across the road.

Song Lee reached for a Kleenex. "Our big old tree doesn't stand tall anymore," she said sadly. "It slumps."

Miss Mackle was the only one who had something nice to say. "It does slump, but there *still* is something to appreciate about that old tree."

Song Lee nodded.

Harry didn't look sad, just thoughtful. "That's like my great-grampa. He can't stand tall either. He has to use a wheelchair now."

"Yes," the teacher agreed. "And there's still a lot to appreciate about your great-grampa, huh?"

"Yeah," Harry agreed. "There sure is!"

Miss Mackle put her hand over her heart as she stared at Harry.

Hanukkah Fun
at Shady Pines

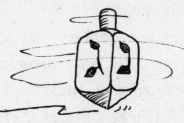

Monday morning, we all walked four blocks up the hill to Shady Pines. Harry and I were partners. It was fun to wear our boots and crunch in the snow.

"It looks like a haunted house," Sid said.

When Harry held up a fist and muttered, "Knock it off, Sid the Squid," I smiled. He was starting to be his old self again.

When we walked into the nursing home, it seemed like we were in someone's living room. There were couches and chairs, and a vase of flowers on a coffee table. A lady at the desk greeted us.

"Good morning, boys and girls. Welcome to Shady Pines. I'm Mrs. Pepper, the administrator."

"Look! They've got a Christmas tree!" Ida exclaimed.

Harry pointed to the dryboard next to it. There were lots of words written in different colors. "See this schedule for December? It tells about all the things going on at Shady Pines. Grampa likes the music programs best because he gets lots of refreshments. He still loves to eat!"

Mrs. Pepper laughed. "Please follow

me to the activity room."

When we got there it was full of elderly people sitting in wheelchairs. "Hi Grampa!" Harry called as he rushed over to him.

Harry kneeled down by his wheelchair and gave him a big hug. "This is my grampa," he said proudly.

"H . . . h . . . hi," Harry's grampa said.

"He stutters now, after his stroke," Harry said matter-of-factly. "This is his roommate Elmer. He wears a bike helmet because he gets seizures sometimes and has to protect his head when he falls."

Mrs. Pepper beamed. "Harry has gotten to know our clients quite well in the past two weeks. He's a regular visitor!"

Mary's mom, Mrs. Berg, patted Harry on the back. She was one of our chaperones.

"Take off your hats and coats, boys and girls," Mrs. Pepper said. "And help yourself to some cocoa and cookies at the refreshment table."

"Thank you!" we said. I took a sugar cookie with rainbow sprinkles.

A lot of the older people spilled cocoa when they drank, but it didn't matter because they were wearing long white bibs.

While people were snacking, Mary's mother announced, "We would like to do an activity with you that we do during Hanukkah. That's a Jewish holiday we usually celebrate in December."

"I know about Hanukkah," a lady said. She was wearing a blonde wig that didn't sit on her head quite right. "I'm Jewish. It's when we celebrate the miracle of the oil lasting eight days in the temple."

"I'm Jewish, too," said a man wearing a blue bow tie. "But my favorite part of Hanukkah is eating fried foods like potato pancakes to remind us of the oil miracle."

"Yes!" Mrs. Berg replied. "The latkes! Mmmmm!

"Our activity is playing the dreidel game. There are four sides to a dreidel," she explained as she handed some to Mary, Ida, and Song Lee to pass out. "Each side has a different Hebrew letter. Together they stand for 'A Great Miracle Happened There.' I'll draw them on this dryboard.

ש

Shin

ח

Hay

ג

Gimmel

נ

Nun

"We learned a song that explains the rules. Ready, boys and girls, to sing?" Mrs. Berg asked.

All of us stopped eating, and sang:

"Oh, dreidel, dreidel, dreidel,
I made it out of clay,
And when my dreidel's ready,
Oh, dreidel I will play.

I'll take my little dreidel
And give it a good strong spin.
I hope it lands on gimmel
For then I'm sure to win.

If I spin hay, I take half,
But none if I spin nun.
I get the pot with gimmel,
With shin I must pay one."

Few of the elderly could clap for us,
but I could tell by their shiny eyes
they enjoyed it. Mary gave each of us
four gold-wrapped chocolate coins
from her basket.

"This is gelt," she said. "What you
put in the pot when you play dreidel."

"Tha-that's like po-po-po-poker,"
Harry's grampa said.

"Yes!" Mary replied.

Harry beamed. "We know how to
play that, huh Grampa!"

"We su-su-sure d-d-do."

Mrs. Berg held up a hand. "Okay!

The students will partner up with people here at Shady Pines. They've been practicing in class, so they know how to play. There's just one more rule. Share your chocolate winnings!"

Harry and I played with his grampa and Elmer at the end of one long table. We each put one piece of gelt in the pot. I spun the dreidel first. "Nun," I groaned.

Elmer adjusted his bike helmet, then spun next. He got nun also.

Harry spun the top for his grampa. "Shin," he said. "You have to put one in." Harry put a candy in the pot for his grampa and then took a turn. He spun the dreidel real hard.

"Gimmel! Yahoo! I take all the candies."

"Sh-sh-sh . . ." his grampa said.

"Yeah, I know, Grampa," Harry replied. "I have to *share* the chocolate winnings!"

After we unwrapped the chocolate and popped some in our mouths, Harry flashed a toothy smile at me and his grampa. It didn't gross me out that his teeth had chocolate on them. It was great to see my buddy smiling again.

After we read stories and poems to the elderly, we danced and sang to Elvis's Christmas music:

Here comes Santa Claus
Here comes Santa Claus
Right down Santa Claus Lane . . .

When it was time to leave Shady Pines, we all said good-bye to our dreidel partners. Harry gave his grampa a big hug. Then he slapped him five.

On our way downhill back to school, I heard Sidney say, "That was no haunted house. Man, that was a fun house!"

Flying High for
Korean New Year's

Tuesday morning when we walked into class, we noticed Song Lee's mom, Mrs. Park, hanging up Korean clothes in front of the blackboard. She also had placed a kite and a board game on the chalk tray.

After the bell rang, Miss Mackle beamed. "Today Mrs. Park is here to help us learn about the Korean New

Year. Song Lee, do you want to help her?"

Song Lee hurried up to the front of the room and hid behind her mother. We didn't see much of her, just her shoes and left ear.

Mrs. Park didn't force Song Lee to talk. Miss Mackle didn't either. Mrs. Park did most of the talking. "I bring board game called *yut* (yoot). Family play game on Korean New Year. It is holiday gift from us to you."

We clapped and cheered as she held up four wooden sticks and a board. "Each stick has four side. Three curve, one flat. You toss stick in air, and hope it land on flat side. When stick land on flat side, you move token on board."

"Dibs on playing with Song Lee!" Harry said jumping out of his seat.

Miss Mackle motioned for Harry to sit down. "Later, Harry. Let's find out more about the Korean New Year."

"Well," Mrs. Park said reaching for the outfit on the hanger. "Children get dressed up in *hanbok*." We all stared at the rainbow-colored suit made out of silk with a short jacket. "I put on Song Lee now."

You could hear a pin drop as we watched Song Lee step into the beautiful costume.

Harry was half off his desk.

"On Korean New Year, we honor ancestor. Children visit old family and bow to show respect," Mrs. Park said. "Girl bow on one knee. Song Lee, please show class."

We watched Song Lee step in front of her mother, bow and kneel on one knee.

"Boy bow on both knee," Mrs. Park explained.

Harry and I immediately tried bowing to each other on both knees. Mary

and Ida bowed to each other on one knee.

"After children bow, old relative give gift."

"The next time I visit Grampa, I'm bowing to him," Harry said.

Miss Mackle put her hand over her heart.

"We also fly kite on New Year," Mrs. Park continued. "I bring one." We all looked at the white kite Song Lee's mother unfolded. It had a hole right in the middle and streaks of red, blue, and green on it. "It is shield kite," she said.

Song Lee peeked at us through the hole. When we saw her eyeball, we all laughed.

At activity time, we took turns playing *yut* and eating rice cakes that Mrs.

Park had steamed in beef broth.

Then Miss Mackle said we could take Song Lee's shield kite out to the playground. Boy, were we all flying high that sunny, windy day!

Secret Santas

The last week of school in December we did activities about Christmas. I didn't know lots of Lebanese people celebrated Christmas, but they do. ZuZu's mother brought in a *bûche de Noël*. It was a Christmas log cake. The chocolate icing was like the bark of a tree, and the powdered sugar was the snow. It was delicious!

We also made wreaths out of pinecones, decorated a class tree, and made up our own lyrics to songs like "Jingle Bells."

Holidays! Holidays!
They're for me and you!
Christmas, Kwanzaa,
Three Kings' Day,
and Ha-nuk-kah too-oo!

But my favorite Christmas activity was the last one we did. Secret Santas. Miss Mackle brought out her glass jar that always sits on her desk. It had pieces of folded paper inside. Each paper had one class name written on it. "I want you to pick a name from this jar so *you* can be the Secret Santa for that person," she said.

"Instead of buying a gift, though," the

teacher continued, "I want you to choose a white elephant from your house, wrap it up, and give it to that person."

ZuZu was the first to ask. "What's a white elephant, Miss Mackle?"

"Anything used that is still good," the teacher explained. "Like a puzzle with all the pieces. Or a toy that isn't broken but that maybe you don't play with anymore. A book you've read that you are willing to part with. White elephants are things like that."

"I get it!" Sid exclaimed. "I think I'll give my family white elephants this year too. I've got lots of them in my room."

Miss Mackle laughed. "The price is right!"

"I know what I can do!" Harry blurted out.

Mary made a face. "It will be something horrible! I know!"

Harry cackled.

ZuZu raised his eyebrows. "Harry gives horrible gifts?"

Everybody nodded.

"Okay boys and girls. Let's begin!" the teacher announced.

Sidney went up and picked a name first. We all knew who it was. He looked right at Mary. "Darn," he said. "I wanted ZuZu's name. I have something made in France at home. His Lebanese Christmas cake was French. He even knows some French, like me."

ZuZu blushed. I think he liked the attention though.

"Remember what I said," Miss Mackle said holding up one finger. "It's a secret."

At recess, Harry and I raced over to the Dumpster and told each other who we had.

"I have Dexter," Harry said.

"I have Song Lee," I said.

"Want to trade names?" Harry whispered. "I have a white elephant that only Song Lee will appreciate."

"Can we?" I whispered back.

"Why not?" Harry said. "Nobody needs to know. We'll keep it a secret."

Harry and I did a pinky finger shake,

which meant we would not tell a soul. Not even his grampa.

"Okay," I said firmly, "our Secret Santas are a sealed secret now!"

The day before vacation everyone brought wrapped gifts to class. We were pretty excited to find out who our Secret Santas were.

Miss Mackle wore a red dress with a holly corsage from ZuZu, and a head-piece that had reindeer antlers from Harry. She had red-and-green striped candy canes for everyone.

While we licked our peppermint treats we watched each other open up our Secret Santa gifts one by one.

"ZuZu," Miss Mackle said, drawing his name from the jar. "Here's your secret Santa present!"

He unwrapped the Christmas paper

carefully, folded it, and even saved the ribbon. When he opened the card it said,

For ZuZu and JouJou, I'm glad you're in our class. Happy Holidays!
Song Lee

Song Lee's face turned red.

ZuZu unwrapped the gift. "Oh, JouJou will love these! Thank you, Song Lee!"

We all stared at the white elephant gift. It was a stack of three colored pet bowls.

Mary's turn was next. "I know this is from Sidney," she groaned. But as soon as she unwrapped the white elephant, her face lit up. " I love it!"

We all leaned forward to see what came out of the tissue paper. It was the doll Sidney had found in his Three Kings' cake. "I thought I should share the good luck," Sid said. "Like that Christmas song says, 'Good will towards men'!"

ZuZu smiled. "That's a really nice gift, Sidney," he said.

Mary jumped up and down. "Thank you! Thank you!"

When I opened my Santa gift from

Ida, I found a real *kufi*. The hat was made out of fabric, not poster paper. "Wow!" I put it on my head right away.

"It belonged to my uncle," Ida said. "He said I could give it to you."

"Thanks, Ida!" I replied adjusting my *kufi*. I felt kind of cool.

Everyone had to wait until the last Secret Santa present was opened to find out what Harry gave Song Lee. I noticed ZuZu was leaning forward to watch her unwrap the gift. He was really curious what kind of horrible gifts Harry gave.

When she lifted the surprise out of the box, she held up a jar filled with green stuff. The hand-printed label said:

Merry Chrismas
Song Lee
I hope you like this
holaday slime.
I sure like you.
                    Harry

As soon as she opened the lid, a terrible odor filled the room.

"It smells!" Dexter said.

"It stinks!" Sid said.

"It's holiday slime!" Harry said. Then he flashed his white teeth. "It's putrid. That's what Grandma says. I *love* that word."

"It's a horrible gift!" Mary groaned.

"Eeeeyeeew," everyone groaned as Song Lee poured a little into the palm of her hand. It landed like a solid puddle. When she put some between her fingers and rubbed it, the slime turned to powder. "Thank you, Harry," Song Lee said. "I remember you made green slime in class last year with cornstarch and water."

"Yup! But this is a special batch I made last summer. Mom let me keep it in one of her leftover Bell jars in the basement. All I had to do was add a little more water."

"No wonder it smells so bad!" Mary gasped. "It's been fermenting for five months!"

ZuZu cringed. "Your holiday slime *is* horrible, Harry."

"Well," Miss Mackle chuckled, " it *is* a festive green for Christmas."

Song Lee didn't moan or groan like

everyone else. She just giggled. "I like it, Harry. It's stinky fun."

"I knew you'd be the only one who would appreciate it," Harry said.

I just smiled.

Harry was back and as horrible as ever!

Holiday Resources

Brady, April A. *Kwanzaa Karamu: Cooking and Crafts for a Kwanzaa Feast*. Minneapolis: Carolrhoda Books, Inc., 1995.

Carlson, Lori Marie. *Hurray for Three Kings' Day*. New York: Morrow Junior Books, 1999.

Chocolate, Debbi. *A Very Special Kwanzaa*. New York: Scholastic Inc., 1996.

Chocolate, Deborah M. Newton. *My First Kwanzaa Book*. New York: Scholastic Inc., 1992.

DuBois, Jill. *Cultures of the World: Korea*. Tarrytown, New York: Marshall Cavendish, 1996.

Grolier Educational Staff. *Fiesta!: Korea*.Connecticut: Marshall Cavendish, 1997.

Jones, Lynda. *Kids around the World Celebrate!: The Best Feasts and Festivals from Many Lands*. New York: John Wiley & Sons, Inc., 1999.

Kimmel, Eric A., editor. *A Hanukkah Treasury*. New York: Henry Holt & Co., 1998.

Kindersley, Barnabas, and Anabel Kindersley. *Celebrations!: Children Just Like Me*. New York: DK Publishing, Inc., 1997.